For Anna, Maya + Alex
may the moon always shine
brightly for you !

Cari Allen

We See the Moon

by Carrie A. Kitze

For the birthparents of my daughters,
to whom I am forever grateful.

C.A.K.

Published by:
EMK Press,
a division of EMK Group, LLC
16 Mt Bethel Road, #219
Warren, NJ 07059
www.emkpress.com

text ©2003 Carrie A. Kitze

illustrations ©2003 Jinshan Painting Academy,
various artists identified under each work.
Cover image: Flying Kites by Wang Changli.

ISBN 0-9726244-0-6
Library of Congress Control Number: 2002095973

1. Intercountry Adoption–Juvenile fiction   2. Adoption–Juvenile fiction   3. Birthparents–Juvenile fiction

First Edition January, 2003
Printed in China

printed on acid free paper
binding reinforced

This book has its foundation in a song my Grandmother sang to me when I was little. She told me that when we were apart, all I needed to do was to look to the moon. It was the same moon she would see, and we would then be together in our hearts. There are many versions of this song, but here is the one she sang:

I See the Moon...

I see the moon and the moon sees me,

Down through the leaves of the old oak tree.

Please let the light that shines on me,

Shine on the one I love.

Over the mountains, over the sea,

I have a love who is waiting for me.

Please let the light that shines on me,

Shine on the one I love.

In China, during the Mid-Autumn Festival, the tradition is to look to the moon to connect with family and loved ones who can't be together. For adoptive children, the moon becomes a private and powerful tool to connect to a part of themselves, their birth families, who are far away.

May this book help children on their journey of discovery...

I was born

in a faraway land,

of parents

with faces in the shadows.

Mother and Child   Wu Shuhong

Celebrating the New Year's Eve   Zhao Longguan

Where are you now?

I may never know you

but I wonder

who you are,

and what you look like.

Extending New Year's Greetings　Chen Furong

Caring for Children   Yao Zhenzhu

Do you wonder too?

The full moon glows

heavy in the night sky.

A beacon of

beauty and truth.

A Small Town in the Snow   Sheng Pu

Childhood Dream   Zhu Xi

Why did you leave me?

Its soft light

filters through rustling leaves,

making shadows

that play on the grass.

Under the Moonlight   Yang Deliang

Around the House   Xu Xiaoxin

Do you remember me?

I think of you

when the moon is round and golden.

During a quiet time,

a peaceful time.

A Silent Night   Cao Xiuwen

Return to her Parents   Cao Xiuwen

Do you think of me?

I know you are always with me.

All I need is to look

at the moon in the night sky

and think of you.

Night in a Snowy Village   Tao Linping

Water Town   Sheng Pu

Are you looking now?

I miss you and wish you could know

that I am happy here.

My journey

has brought me home.

Releasing Homing Pigeons   Shao Qihua

Family Husbandry   Ruan Sidi

To a place I never would have imagined.

Filled with warmth and love.

I love others now,

And I will always love you.

Resources for Parents:

Talking openly with your children about their adoptive history builds a bond and trust that will last a lifetime. Starting when your child is young makes adoption language commonplace and their story a personal and evolving part of them.

Many of the questions raised in this book will be without answers. We as parents want to have answers to give to our children and may feel uncomfortable when we don't. What is interesting is that our children don't feel the same way. Adult adoptees have expressed a sadness in not knowing the answers, but the larger sadness is in feeling that they were unable to actually ask the questions without hurting their parents.

For more information on these issues, Jane Brown, an adoption social worker, adoptive parent of children from Korea and China, and member of the advisory board of Adoptive Families Magazine, has prepared a user guide to help parents and children. It is available on our website (www.emkpress.com) or via mail by sending a stamped, self addressed #10 envelope to EMK Press, 16 Mt. Bethel Road #219, Warren, NJ 07059.

Create a Lifebook:

A project you can do with your child to talk about the unanswered questions this book raises is to create a Lifebook. Different from a scrapbook, this is a child's history from birth with places for them to draw pictures and talk about their feelings. For a great resource on creating one, get *LifeBooks: Creating a Treasure for the Adopted Child*, by Beth O'Malley M.Ed, or visit her website: www.adoptionlifebooks.com.

About the paintings:

Jinshan Peasant Paintings are created by Chinese peasants working in Jinshan County near Shanghai, China. During the late 1970s, the Chinese painter Wu Tongzhang began teaching painting techniques to the farmers in Jinshan. Most of these first painters were older women skilled in various folk arts that had been passed down through generations. All the paintings represented here were painted by Artists at the Jinshan Peasant Painting Academy. They use tempera paint mixed with chalk, and paint on xuan (rice) paper. The paintings are then attached to heavier paper. The use of bright colors and limited use of perspective gives these paintings a primitive, childlike quality. For more information visit www.chinesefolkart.com.

Help those left behind:

A portion of the proceeds from this book help children remaining in orphanages throughout the world. We sponsor children in foster care programs through Holt International. Visit www.holtintl.org for information on becoming a sponsor. Children in many countries could use your help. We also donate money for scholarships for orphanage children to gain an education in China. We use Families with Children from China Orphanage Assistance Programs (www.fccny.org). This program partners primarily with The Amity Foundation, a highly respected Chinese non-profit, non-governmental agency in Nanjing.

Visit our website (www.emkpress.com) to find more links and resources for parents and to learn more about the children who receive aid thanks to the proceeds from this book.